Oxford University Press, Walton Street, Oxford OX2 6DP

Oxford New York
Athens Auckland Bangkok Bombay
Calcutta Cape Town Dar es Salaam Delhi
Florence Hong Kong Istanbul Karachi
Kuala Lumpur Madras Madrid Melbourne
Mexico City Nairobi Paris Singapore
Taipei Tokyo Toronto

and associated companies in
Berlin Ibadan

Oxford is a trade mark of Oxford University Press

© Victor and Glenys Ambrus 1995
First published 1995
ISBN 0 19 279941 X (hardback)
ISBN 0 19 272228 X (paperback)

A CIP catalogue record for this book is available
from the British Library

Printed in Hong Kong

Santa Claus Snowed Under!

Victor and
Glenys Ambrus

Oxford University Press

OXFORD TORONTO MELBOURNE

Santa Claus made himself a mug of hot chocolate, sat in his favourite armchair in front of the television, and waited for the weather forecast.

'Snow, snow, and more snow!' said the weatherman. 'Villages all over the country are cut off. Stay indoors and keep warm!'

'I should be so lucky!' said Santa. 'I've got work to do!'

He turned off the television and went outside to give the reindeer in the barn an extra large feed of oats.

'You're going to need this!' he said.

The sleigh was piled high with presents and ready for take off.

Deep in the countryside a small school was now completely cut off by snow. The children couldn't get home and the rescue service couldn't reach them.

'The food is running low,' complained the cook. 'If help doesn't come soon, there'll be nothing to eat!'

The children had huge snowfights, skated on the frozen-over swimming-pool, and built an enormous snowman.

Not many miles away, Sunnydene Retirement Home was also cut off by snow. The central heating system had broken down and the old people kept warm by doing exercises and wrapping themselves in blankets. They sang songs to keep cheerful and had extra games of bingo.

'I'm sick of bingo,' moaned one lady to her friend.

Meanwhile, Santa had started his rounds. He flew over snowed-up lorries, dropping presents to surprised lorry-drivers huddled round bonfires.

The extra oats had worked and the reindeer pulled so well that by eleven o'clock nearly all the presents had been delivered.

'Nearly finished!' Santa sighed, as he stopped at a huge Gothic mansion. He slid down the chimney into a room filled with television sets. In front of them sat Mr Diamond, the reclusive multi-millionaire.

'I'm really stumped!' said Santa. 'What can I give the man who has everything?'

'I'd just like some cheerful company,' answered the millionaire gloomily. 'The cook's miserable—she's made loads of delicious food and there's no one to eat it! The butler's miserable—no one to wait on. The only one who's happy is the weatherman!'

Fifty weathermen were grinning away and warning everyone of more blizzards.

'I'll see what I can do,' promised Santa.

'That's one place I've not been to,' he said as he spotted lights down below. He landed in front of the school and saw all the children playing.

'Why aren't you in bed?' Santa asked.

'There's no food left,' said the head-teacher, 'and the children are too hungry to sleep.'

'Everyone jump up on my sleigh,' said Santa. 'I know where there's lots of food! But first let's go to Sunnydene.'

When Santa and his passengers arrived, the old people were still awake.

'They were all too cold to sleep,' the matron told Santa.

'Everyone on to the sleigh!' shouted Santa. 'I know just the place to have a good warm.'

In no time at all the old people and the children were whizzed through the blizzard and landed outside the millionaire's mansion.

The butler, hearing singing, thought some carol singers were lost in the snow.

'Come in, come in,' he beamed. Everyone trooped into the warm hall.

The butler announced that Christmas dinner
was served. Everyone sat down at the enormous table
in the dining room and ate all the good food the cook had made.
    'Speech, speech!' called someone.
    Mr Diamond stood up. 'You are most welcome, dear friends,'
he said. 'My home is your home.'

'We'll take you up on that!' cried one old man. 'Our lease is up next month!'

'Brilliant!' said Mr Diamond, the butler, and the cook together.

'Diamond is a girl's best friend,' sang two old ladies.

The cook was overjoyed—all those hungry people to enjoy her cooking.

'Now everyone is happy,' smiled Santa, as he watched Mr Diamond waltz with one of the old ladies from Sunnydene.

The party continued after dinner until worried parents arrived with the rescue team.

'I don't know what you were worrying about,' said one child, 'we were having a lovely time!'

The children were taken home, but the old people stayed on.

Santa was soon back in his armchair. He turned on the television, just in time to catch the weather forecast.

'Reports are coming in of an old man with a white beard, using a sleigh to rescue stranded people—it's enough to make you believe in Santa Claus! Ha! Ha!'

'There's one born every minute!' said Santa.